Divya Dubey

To the friendships that nourish me, and to Zayden, Kayshan, and Saya ♡
—S.J.

Published by Stone Arch Books, an imprint of Capstone
1710 Roe Crest Drive, North Mankato, Minnesota 56003
capstonepub.com

Text copyright © 2025 by Sita Jit
Illustrations copyright © 2025 by Capstone

All rights reserved. No part of this publication may be reproduced in whole or in part, or stored in a retrieval system, or transmitted in any form or by any means, electronic, mechanical, photocopying, recording, or otherwise, without written permission of the publisher.

Library of Congress Cataloging-in-Publication Data
is available on the Library of Congress website.
ISBN: 9781669078036 (hardcover)
ISBN: 9781669078043 (paperback)
ISBN: 9781669078098 (ebook PDF)

Summary: When a family friend asks to have her mehndi party at Divya's family's restaurant, Divya knows just how to decorate to make the party truly magical. But none of the adults will listen to her ideas. So she makes a plan to show her family how responsible she is. Will she prove herself, or will her plan be a total disaster?

Design Elements
Getty Images: Iuliia Mashinets, star design element throughout, krishnapriya, design element pattern throughout

Designer: Elijah Blue

Printed and bound in the USA. 6121

Divya's Supersecret Plan

written by **Sita Jit**
illustrated by **Abhilasha Khatri**

STONE ARCH BOOKS
a capstone imprint

Chapter 1

Party Planning

Do you have two homes? I do. One home is far, far away, in Delhi, India, where I was born and lived most of my life. A home that I love and miss. The second is here, in this new country, surrounded by tall towers and a family I moved in with a few months ago who are also pretty nice.

Let me tell you about it. Mumma, Papa, and I left our life back home in India. It was hard to say goodbye to my nani, my mumma's mumma, who I miss terribly. And of course, the friends I left behind.

We flew halfway around the world to be closer to Dadi, my papa's mumma. Mumma and Papa also wanted to help Taya Ji, my papa's older brother, and Tayi Ji, his wife, with the family restaurant, Delhi Delights.

My uncle and aunty have two kids, my cousins Geeta Didi and Sumeer. Geeta Didi is in the sixth grade, and we share a bedroom. We got off to a rocky start but are closer than ever now. Sumeer is in the fourth grade like me, but we are in different classes.

We all live together in an apartment above Delhi Delights, the most magical restaurant with the most delicious food from all around India. Speaking of Delhi Delights, that's where the story of my supersecret plan begins.

We were sitting in Delhi Delights, having our usual weekend afternoon chai and biscuits. Soft sounds of classical Indian music played through the speakers.

Dadi was taking a sip of her steaming chai and reading her Indian newspaper. My cousin Geeta Didi nibbled on biscuits and scrolled on her phone. My cousin Sumeer dipped his biscuit into his warm cup of milk. Mumma, Papa, Taya, and Tayi Ji were sitting and chatting.

My superspecial notebook sat open in front of me. You see, I love making lists and writing my secrets down, so I take it everywhere! I especially enjoy adding to the list of things I love.

Things I love:

☆ This notebook of course!
☆ Basketball, my favorite sport
☆ Orange and other bright colors

- ☆ Ladoos—the most delicious round balls of goodness that crumble in my mouth with each bite
- ☆ Nani, who is in India
- ☆ The times the restaurant is quiet and we are all together

I heard a loud screech from a chair being pushed back. I put my pencil down and looked at Taya Ji. I was used to seeing him smiling or laughing, usually at his own bad jokes, but today he was extra smiley, even for him!

"Family, can I get your attention?" Taya Ji stood up and cleared his throat. He smiled so bright I could see all his teeth. "We have some exciting news! We all know our most special customer, Ms. Simran, yes? She comes most Sundays for lunch."

We all nodded our heads.

I loved Simran Aunty! Everyone said that

she and I looked like sisters with our short, wavy, dark hair and oversized glasses. I loved when they said that because she was so nice, and I loved chatting with her about my week at school. My insides bubbled. She was my absolute favorite customer!

Taya Ji's voice interrupted my thoughts. "Ms. Simran is getting married in a few weeks and has asked us to host her first wedding function! Delhi Delights will be closing to our guests for the very first time and hosting our first ever, very special mehndi party for a most special bride-to-be, Ms. Simran. It is the highest honor. Since her family is back in Punjab, Ms. Simran has left the planning to us."

I looked up in surprise! I knew Simran Aunty was getting married, but I never dreamed she would have one of her traditional wedding functions at the restaurant!

Ahhhhh! I'm sooo excited! And my favorite function. A mehndi party!

I *loved* mehndi parties. Back in India we went to so many! They were when the bride-to-be had red-orange mehndi applied to her palms, back of her hands, and feet. The guests also got to join in the fun with mehndi designs for themselves, lively music, delicious food, and nonstop dancing.

But the bright colors and decorations at mehndi parties were my favorite part. I couldn't wait to tell everyone everything I knew to help make this party extra special for Simran Aunty.

Dadi clapped her hands in front of her. "Oh, how wonderful! She is such a sweet girl. Always says, 'namaste' and asks about my health. We must make this very special for her."

Tayi Ji nodded. "We will of course make sure we have the most delicious food ready for her guests. Our restaurant already looks great, so we can completely focus on the food. The menu will be perfect! That is what everyone will be talking about."

I looked around at the restaurant. Square wooden tables and fancy cushioned chairs filled the room. The walls were powder blue and had pictures of India on them. It was a beautiful restaurant, but mehndi parties had to be *extra* special.

Before I knew it, words were spilling out of my mouth. "The decorations at the restaurant are very good, but for this special event, maybe we can do something a bit more special. You know, like we do in India? Maybe some colorful dupattas on the wall, as well as something special for the tables?"

I looked up expecting them to clap at my brilliant ideas, or at least be taking notes. But no. Mumma, Papa, Dadi, Taya Ji, and Tayi Ji were already sitting together and talking about if samosa or pakora should be served as snacks. Tayi Ji had her notepad and was making a list of dishes. Almost like I never said anything at all!

I shrunk back in my chair and folded my arms over my chest.

"Good try, Divya," Sumeer said patting my shoulder. He pushed back his chair and stood up. "You had a good idea, but I guess the adults have other things to worry about. I'm going to take this as my cue to leave. There is a video game waiting for me."

He walked out of the restaurant.

Geeta Didi put her phone down and turned toward me. "I like your ideas. I haven't been to many mehndi parties, but it sounds like a lot of work. Why don't you just leave it up to the adults? I mean, that's what I'm going to do."

"I know. It's just that Simran Aunty is so nice, and I really want this celebration to be

special for her. I've been to so many mehndi parties in India, and they were magical. I felt like I was transported to a beautiful place each time. I really want that for her," I said.

"Maybe you can try talking to them later?" Geeta Didi said as she pushed her chair back and turned to leave.

I nodded and got up to go. I turned to look at Taya Ji, Tayi Ji, Dadi, Mumma, and Papa. There was still lots of time to change their minds.

Note to self:

☆ Mehndi parties are the best!

☆ When adults don't listen to kids, it is the worst!

Chapter 2

The Idea

Mumma, Papa, Taya Ji, Tayi Ji, and Dadi spent most of Saturday going back and forth with ideas for the menu for the party. Each time I tried to get Mumma and Papa alone, they said, "Not now, Divya. We have so much to do. We will talk soon."

Finally, on Sunday after breakfast, Papa and Mumma walked into the bedroom I shared with Geeta Didi. "Is this a good time to talk, Divya?" Papa asked as he sat at the edge of my bed. Mumma stood beside him.

"Yeah, Geeta Didi has gone for a walk with Dadi," I said. "I can finally talk to you about my mehndi party ideas."

Mumma and Papa looked at each other, their eyebrows raised. I took this as a good sign and continued the speech I had practiced in my head since yesterday.

"Do you remember the time when we were back home in India and I wanted to paint my bedroom orange, and you didn't think it was a good idea, but I did it anyway?"

Mumma and Papa weren't too happy to find me covered in paint along with splashes of paint on my brand-new rug. Maybe this story wasn't such a good idea.

Mumma nodded cautiously. "Where are you going with this story, Divya?"

"At first you were upset that I didn't listen to you, but then you admitted that my room looked great."

"Yes, we remember," Papa said. He turned to Mumma, his eyebrows nearly touching the ceiling. Mumma shrugged her shoulders, a confused look on her face.

Why were Mumma and Papa looking at each other like that? My cheeks grew warm. All the ideas I carefully practiced seemed so jumbled up now.

"Well, kids can also have good ideas that sometimes adults don't listen to," I said fast before I lost my courage.

Papa got up from the side of the bed and walked over to me. "Yes, of course, beta. But what does this have to do with the orange walls? Are you planning on painting this room?"

I shook my head. This wasn't going so well. I tried again.

"Yesterday, when we were talking about Simran Aunty's mehndi party, I suggested we decorate the restaurant to make it extra

special," I explained. "But no one listened to my great ideas."

Papa and Mumma looked at each other knowingly. Finally! My body felt like it was melting like butter. My beating heart slowed down a bit.

"Oh, that's right. I think we got so busy with planning the menu. I understand you may want to help, but the decor at the restaurant already looks great. We should focus on the menu. After all, that is what the guests will be talking about." Papa began to list all the dishes that would be made for the special event.

My cheeks flushed. I folded my arms across my chest and tapped my feet as Papa listed each dish.

When he finally finished, my words were angry. "Papa, that's great. But just listen to me. I thought maybe we could have some decorations on the wall, some trinkets on the table. Maybe even diyas! It will be beautiful. I know Simran Aunty and all her guests would love it."

Papa looked down at his watch. "Beta, we have to get down to the restaurant. We can talk more about this later."

My shoulders fell. I looked down at my feet.

"I know you want to help, Divya. But it's best to leave the planning to the adults," Papa said just before he rushed toward the door.

Mumma nodded. "Beta, we know you want to help, but this is our first mehndi party in this country. Let's see how this goes and maybe we can use your ideas in the next one." She kissed my cheek before she walked out the door behind Papa.

My body felt hot all the way down to my toes. When did my parents stop listening to me?

Note to self:

☆ Maybe reminding my parents about the orange paint wasn't such a good idea.

☆ Guests can care about food *and* decorations.

The bedroom was quiet now that Mumma and Papa had left. My cheeks were still flushed, and my heart was still beating quickly. I picked up my notebook from the table beside my bed. Drawing helped calm my nerves.

I began sketching the restaurant, and my ideas for the mehndi party decorations poured out of me.

Half an hour later, I put my pencil down and looked at my creation. The page was filled with tables decorated with bangles, candles, colorful tablecloths, and plates.

The walls behind the special bride-to-be chair were covered in soft, colorful fabrics and filled with cushions. The designs looked perfect. This is what Simran Aunty's party should look like! If only I could create this in real life!

I tapped my pencil against my notebook.

But wait! What if I *could* create this in real life? And surprise the adults! Like the most supersecret plan that would blow everyone away. They would love it so much and then I could help with the mehndi party!

I wrote out my ideas to make my supersecret plan a reality.

Divya's Supersecret Plan

⭐ Step 1:
   Design

☆ Step 2:
   Collect dupattas, diyas, bangles, and more!

☆ Step 3:
   Set up the decorations in the dining room to show everyone how fabulous my ideas are, blow them away, knock their socks off, surprise them until they love my ideas!
   A mini mehndi party!

Step one was easy and done. Now on to step two. Where would I find everything I needed?

I looked around my room. There wasn't much here to help me. The purple walls weren't my favorite, but I liked them now. The basketball poster above my bed didn't fit the theme. The closet I shared with Geeta Didi was filled with clothing. The shimmery fabric of my salwar kameez hanging in my closet sparkled.

Aha! I've got it!

I jumped up off my bed and reached for the sequined green dupatta. It was perfect!

Geeta Didi walked through the door. "Dadi is the fastest walker ever! I'm tired." She plopped down on her bed. "How are you doing, Divya? Did you get to talk to your parents about the mehndi party?"

I turned to face her, my pink salwar kameez in hand.

"I did, but it didn't go so well," I said as I pulled the lace dupatta off the hanger and placed the salwar kameez back in the closet. "They basically said I should leave all the planning to the adults."

Geeta Didi sat up. "I know that's not what you wanted to hear. Are you okay?" She looked at the dupatta in my hands and raised her eyebrow in question.

"I'm good! Do you have any bright dupattas? I came up with the best idea! It's actually my supersecret plan. I'm not telling anyone but you, and maybe my new best friend Asima."

Geeta Didi leaned in closer toward me. "Oh, I love supersecret plans. What were you thinking?"

"I'm going to recreate this design for the adults and actually show them how great my ideas are. There is no way they can ignore me then." I placed the bright dupatta on the bed and held up the sketch in my notebook.

She jumped off the bed and stood beside me. She took my notebook and stared at the pages for what seemed like forever.

"Well . . . what do you think? I mean, it's a rough sketch but will look better in person. I just need to find everything and . . . ," I trailed off. Why was she taking so long to answer? Maybe my idea wasn't so good.

"This is amazing, Divya! I love it. I can't believe you drew this! Let me see what I can find. But are you sure about this?" she asked as she moved clothes around in her closet.

"I know adults don't usually like surprises. They like to think they are always right."

"Yeah, that's true, but this time, I know I am right." I waved my hands in front of the dupattas on my bed. "These are my dupattas, and with yours I'll have enough for my plan."

My tummy fluttered with excitement. "I'm so excited. The mehndi parties I used to go to in India were even more beautiful. I really want to help make this day so special for Simran Aunty."

Geeta Didi walked over to my bed and dropped three brightly colored dupattas. One pink laced, another that was fiery red, and the last one a shimmery green with tiny crystals. "These are my favorite so please take good care of them," she said.

"I'll take *extra* great care of them! Thank you, Geeta Didi," I said giving her my most dazzling smile.

Note to self:

☆ Dupattas are magical!

☆ I can't wait for everyone to see how beautiful my decorations will be!

Chapter 3

The Class Fundraiser

". . . and they didn't listen to a thing I had to share," I told my best friend Asima. I hung my backpack on the chair in our fourth-grade classroom and sat down at my desk. Asima sat beside me in her usual spot.

"Sometimes it feels like no one listens to me in our busy house or takes me seriously. Even my parents! It never used to be like this in India," I said. I took my orange pencil case from my backpack.

"Divya, that's a lot. What will you do?" Asima said. She put her books into her desk.

Ms. Yang, our fourth-grade teacher, sat at the front grading papers. My classmates chatted around us. I looked up at the clock. The bell should ring any minute, so I had to be quick.

I reached into my backpack and pulled out my notebook. I turned to the page with my drawing and the page with my step-by-step plan.

"This is my supersecret plan. I'm going to show the adults that they were wrong by setting up a mini mehndi party in the dining room next weekend. Simran Aunty's party could use some color and fun!"

"Ooh, so colorful! Let me know how I can help, Divya," she squealed.

"I will. Once I know when I will set this up," I said.

Asima nodded vigorously. It felt good knowing my best friend believed in me, just like Geeta Didi.

Ms. Yang looked at the clock. She pushed her chair back from her desk just as the bell rang.

"Class, I need you to settle down quickly. We have a special guest this morning."

On cue, Mr. Khan, the school principal, walked into the room and stood beside Ms. Yang. Mr. Khan always wore funny ties that matched his socks. Today was no different. Red and yellow fish swam across his chest and around his ankles.

"Mr. Khan is here to share some very exciting news," Ms. Yang said before stepping aside to let Mr. Khan speak.

Mr. Khan cleared his throat. His deep voice filled the room. "Thank you, Ms. Yang. I am excited to share that our annual Family Fun night is fast approaching. This year, each class will be fundraising for something special. We decided to create an outdoor classroom.

The space will allow for important learning to take place in the beautiful outdoors of our schoolyard. Each class will participate by creating a special fundraiser. It could be anything, making something to sell, creating cards, anything really."

A loud "hooray" nearly escaped from my mouth. I covered it before Ms. Yang looked my way. She liked it when we were serious, especially around Mr. Khan.

Most days in India, our class would work outside under the shade of the large trees that surrounded our school. Some of my favorite memories were of reading and writing in my notebook outside.

"This is the best news ever!" I whispered to Asima.

Asima nodded. She kept her eyes on Ms. Yang. Ms. Yang was staring straight at me and giving me the *stop talking, Divya* look. You know, the one where your teacher's eyes look straight at you. They don't blink or smile. Not even one bit.

I took my fingers and pulled them across my lips like I was zipping my mouth shut. She finally looked away.

"Family Fun night is in two weeks. Each class will decide how they will fundraise. So, take some time and think of ways your class will participate. Ms. Yang can answer any questions you may have," Mr. Khan clapped his hands in front of him. "On to the next class. I look forward to seeing what you decide."

As he left and walked out the door, I turned to Asima. "This is the best news! I have so many ideas! Maybe we can have a clothing swap, or sell daffodils, or a bake sale, or maybe we can . . ."

I got so caught up in my ideas that I didn't notice Asima's raised eyebrows and fingers pointing behind me.

"Ahem. I hope I'm not interrupting you too much, Divya. It sounds like you have many ideas, but let's see what others have to say," Ms. Yang said sternly.

My cheeks flushed. This was the second time in three days when I had ideas but no one would listen to me. First my family, and now my teacher!

"Of course, Ms. Yang. Sorry." I slouched back in my chair. Ms. Yang walked to the front and turned toward the class.

"I know you must all have lots of ideas," she said. "So, let's share them and then we can vote on what our class would like to do. I'll write your thoughts on the board."

My friend, Jamal, who sat in front of Asima and me, raised his hand. Ms. Yang picked up the dry-erase marker and called on him. "How about selling chocolates? My cousin's school did that, and they raised lots of money."

"That's great. Let me write that down," Ms. Yang said.

My classmates shared their ideas while I looked out the window. The schoolyard had an empty space between the playground, the basketball court, and the field. Maybe that was where the outdoor classroom would go. Right next to the large trees.

"Divya," Ms. Yang said. I sat up straight and looked at her like I had been paying attention the whole time. What could I have done wrong now? Was I getting in trouble for not talking? Is that even allowed?

"Divya, you had some thoughts earlier. Is there anything you'd like to add to our list?"

I sat up even straighter and scanned the list quickly.

"Umm . . . how about a bake sale?" I said. "Maybe one where we bring in our family's traditional food, things we love to eat or are special to us."

Asima nodded. "Yes, that's a great idea, Divya," she said enthusiastically.

Ms. Yang added my idea to the list. My heart soared. It felt good to have my ideas heard.

"This looks like a great list. Time to vote by secret ballot," Ms. Yang announced. "I'll count up the votes and announce the winner just before recess."

My tummy fluttered. The more I thought about the bake sale, the more excited I got. After I finished my math worksheet, I began making a list of my favorite Indian sweets I wanted to make.

☆ Ladoo

☆ Jalebi

☆ Halwa

Just as I finished writing the last item on my list, Ms. Yang announced, "It looks like we have a winner. We will be having a bake sale! Over the next few days, think about what you would like to bring for the sale. We will have a sign-up sheet later this week."

I jumped up out of my seat and shouted, "Hooray!" My cheeks flushed when I noticed everyone looking at me. I sat down fast and zipped my lips before Ms. Yang could say anything.

Ms. Yang looked at me and smiled. "Let's thank Divya for the great idea."

Note to self:

☆ "Let's thank Divya for the great idea" sounds soooo good!

☆ It feels nice to have someone listen to me for a change.

Chapter 4

The Plan

"Our class is going to have a bake sale! Can you believe it! It was actually my idea. It will be great. I just can't wait!" The words ran quickly from my mouth as Sumeer, Geeta Didi, and I walked home from school.

"Divya, slow down! I have no idea what you are saying," Sumeer said.

"Sumeer, I thought you would be used to Divya's speedy words by now. I, on the other hand, understood everything," Geeta Didi said. She ruffled her younger brother's curly hair and repeated what I said.

I laughed. Back in India, everyone always said I spoke really quickly. The good news was that I talked fast in all the countries I lived in.

"Geeta Didi, no wonder you understand Divya," said Sumeer. "Since she got here, you've started to talk faster too!"

Geeta Didi chuckled. "I guess I have." She winked at me. "You are rubbing off on me, little cousin."

"I guess I am." I winked back. "It's time for you to join the fast-talkers club too, Sumeer."

"I'll try my best to keep up with you both." He laughed. "Do you know what you want to make for the bake sale, Divya?"

"I had a few ideas, but what I think I really want to make are my nani's ladoos. Back in India, when Nani made them, the whole neighborhood would stop by for a taste."

"I can't wait to try them. I can be the official taste tester!" Sumeer announced.

"For sure!" I laughed. "What are your classes doing?" I asked my cousins.

"Our class decided that we will make greeting cards and sell them," Summer said. "I'm going to draw my favorite cars. Who doesn't love cars?"

"That sounds really cool and creative. How about you Geeta Didi?" I turned to her. She seemed to be dragging her feet beside me.

"Ugh. My class will be having a danceathon and collecting donations," she replied. "It wasn't my first choice. But I guess it's fine." She pushed her hair over her shoulder.

"Maybe you'll like it more than you think. I just know I can't wait!" I said.

Geeta Didi and Sumeer were used to fundraisers. We didn't have anything like this back in India, so I couldn't wait for Family Fun night.

I skipped the rest of the way home.

Note to self:

☆ Learn how to make Nani's ladoos.

☆ Outdoor classrooms are the best!

☆ So are Family Fun nights!

At dinner, I couldn't wait to tell everyone the exciting news. "You all have to come to my first ever Family Fun night! Our class is doing a bake sale, and it was my idea!" I said, my mouth moving quickly. "I'm making my nani's ladoos! They will be delicious!"

Dadi's face lit up. "Oh, that is marvelous, beta. We will be there." The adults all nodded.

"Divya, if you need any help making the ladoos, I'm happy to assist," Tayi Ji said.

"I can help too," Dadi said. She looked at me with her kind eyes and soft smile.

"Thank you, but I have decided I really want to make them on my own. I am very responsible and can do this by myself."

Papa put his hands on my shoulders. "Beta, we know you are responsible and can do this on your own. We are happy to help."

"I know," I said. I put his hand in mine and gave it a squeeze. "I'll let you know if I need anything. I am somewhat of a ladoo expert as they are my favorite food. I just know they will be delicious and perfect," I said. I took a bite of my soft aloo paratha.

Sumeer looked around the table. "I can't think of anyone better than Divya to make ladoos. I mean, no one in the world loves ladoos as much as she does. What can go wrong?"

I looked up at everyone with a grin and nodded. "I agree with Sumeer! What could go wrong?"

After supper, the adults returned to Delhi Delights for the dinner rush. Dadi had gone to her room to rest, leaving Geeta Didi, Sumeer, and me to clear the table.

With the excitement of the mehndi party and Family Fun night coming up in less than two weeks, my mind started racing. I came up with the *best* idea! Now that I was making ladoo for the bake sale, it would be my second chance to impress the adults!

First with my decorations and second with my cooking skills! I pulled out my notebook and added to my supersecret plan. My party was going to be a huge success!

Divya's Supersecret Plan

⭐ Step 1:
  Design

☆ Step 2:
  Collect dupattas, diyas, bangles, and more!

☆ Step 3:
  Make delicious ladoos all by myself on the same day and set up the decorations in the dining room to show everyone how fabulous my ideas are, blow them away, knock their socks off, surprise them until they love my ideas and cooking!

A mehndi party with food! *Who doesn't love a good party?!* I thought.

"Divya, what are you up to? You have a silly grin on your face," Geeta Didi said.

A half plate of rice sat balanced in her hands.

I quickly wiped the grin off my face and mumbled, "Nothing," and walked toward the kitchen.

My mind was working overtime. If I could make a batch of ladoo for my family next weekend, I could show them how responsible I was *and* decorate this dining room with my ideas for the mehndi party. There is *no* way that they will be able to turn down my ideas now.

Note to self:

☆ I can't wait to put my double perfect plan into action!

☆ I am full of great ideas today!

Chapter 5

Finally Friday

After a long week of reading, writing, science, math, and more, it was finally Friday. I got to school extra early and couldn't wait for my day to start. Especially the part where we signed up for the treats we would make!

The morning went so slowly! Finally, right before recess, Ms. Yang stood up from her desk with a large sheet of paper in her hands and walked toward the board.

"Before you go out for recess, please sign up for what you will be bringing to the bake sale. I'd like to have this complete by the end of the day," Ms. Yang said. She taped the paper on the board just as the bell rang.

I pushed my chair back and jumped up. "I'm ready to sign up! I'm ready! I'm going to make my nani's ladoos! She is mumma's mumma, lives in India, and makes the best food! It's a special family recipe."

I rushed to the front and grabbed the marker. Ms. Yang stepped out of the way just in time.

"Slow down, Divya! You can go first, just don't knock me over." She laughed.

I turned to see Asima and Jamal close behind me. The rest of the class went out for recess.

I scribbled ladoo next to my name before anyone else could take my idea.

Once I was done, I put the cap back on the marker and handed it to Asima.

"What are you bringing?" I asked. "You already know what I'm bringing."

She uncapped the marker. "I'm bringing ma'amoul. It's my favorite cookie and reminds me of being back home in Syria. We used to have it every week. Baba and I are going to make it together for the sale. It will be delicious."

I wrapped my arms around her and gave her the warmest hug. "I can't wait to try your homemade food."

She smiled and hugged me back. "And I can't wait to try yours!"

Jamal took the marker as Asima put it back on the ledge of the whiteboard.

"I'm going to be the first in line to try both your treats," he said. "I'm bringing my family's delicious coconut drops. *Mmmm,* they are sooo good."

My excitement exploded. "Ohhh, I can't wait, Jamal!"

My two friends were bringing in treats I'd never tried before. This would be the best bake sale ever!

After recess, we sat at our desks. Ms. Yang cleared her throat. "For our art class today, we will be making posters for our bake sale and post them around the school. Since our fundraiser is next Friday, we have five school days until Family Fun night to build up the excitement."

She held up large rectangular sheets of poster paper. "Remember to make your work bright and eye-catching."

Asima and I turned and grinned at each

other. We loved to draw. And the brighter the better for me!

"Ms. Yang, since the paper is bigger than our desk, can a few of us work in the hallway? You know how much I love to spread out on the floor when I draw," I said.

Ms. Yang put her hands on her hips. "As long as you promise not to talk. The last time you were out there, other teachers complained and I had to call you back in."

"I promise!" I began pushing in my chair, "I'll be as quiet as a mouse!"

Ms. Yang agreed to let Asima and Jamal work in the hallway too. They followed me outside.

I lay down with my tummy on the floor and began by making large bubble letters with pencil. I was doing my best to be as quiet as possible. Ten minutes later I was itching to talk. Once I finished making my round ladoo, I grabbed the dark yellow

marker. "This isn't the exact color of my nani's ladoos, but it will have to do. How are you both doing with your work?" My promise to stay quiet was forgotten.

I sat up and crossed my legs beside my friends. I looked at their posters and loved what I saw.

"Jamal, I love your poster! The coconut drops look delicious enough to eat! How did you pick what you would bring?"

Jamal looked around, and there were no teachers in sight. "Every summer we go to Jamaica to visit my granny and granddad. Granny and I always make our coconut gumdrops together. They are sweet, chewy, and taste like toffee. It's our special thing," he whispered.

I squeezed my lips together, so I wouldn't squeal with excitement. I loved trying new food. After taking three deep breaths, I whispered, "Oh, I love that, Jamal. I should have made ladoos with my nani when I was in India. I guess I was just too busy eating them. I wish I had. I feel so far away from her." I looked down at my poster.

"Divya, your nani will be so happy you are going to make her ladoos. I'm sure it will help you feel closer to her," Jamal whispered back.

Asima nodded. Her voice was quiet but loud enough for Jamal and me to hear her words. "I agree with Jamal. My baba and I will make ma'amoul together just like we used to. He has to work a lot since we moved here so baking together reminds me of happy times before we had to leave. I love that our food reminds us of the people and places we love."

I loved my friends and I loved what made them special. I looked down at our posters. One with ladoos, one with coconut gumdrops, and one with ma'amoul.

<u>Note to self:</u>

☆ Food stories can connect us.

☆ I hope everyone loves our treats!

After school, just as our class packed up to leave, Asima said, "Have a good weekend, Divya."

I could hardly believe how quickly the week had passed. "Thanks, Asima! It will be busy. I have so much to do," I said as I shoved my books into my backpack.

"That's right!" Asima said. "This is the big weekend you are making ladoo and setting up the decorations for the mini mehndi party!"

"Yup! It is! I'm so excited, and I just know everything will be perfect. But I have a lot of work to do." I held my blue notebook tightly in my hands.

"Well, my offer to help still stands. I can come over if you need me. I don't have much to do on Sunday," Asima said. We walked toward the door.

I opened my notebook and scanned my to-do list:

☆ talk to Nani and get her ladoo recipe
☆ go to the store to buy what I need for ladoo and decorations
☆ make ladoo
☆ set up the decor

These are all big jobs! A bead of sweat began forming on my forehead. Maybe having some help with the decorations wouldn't hurt.

"Asima, I would love that. How about

you come over at three on Sunday and you can help me decorate? I will be making the ladoo all by myself before you come. Will that work for you?"

"I'll ask my baba. I think it should be fine," she said just as we got to the front of the school.

I waved to her as she got into her baba's car. Once she left, I joined Sumeer and Geeta Didi, who were waiting for me.

Note to self:

☆ This weekend has to go perfectly!

☆ I can't wait to talk to Nani tomorrow! Woo-hoo!

Chapter 6
The Ladoo Recipe

BRRRIIINGG!

My eyes popped open with the sound of the alarm clock on Saturday morning. I sat up and looked toward Geeta Didi's empty bed. My video call with Nani was in twenty minutes. I had just enough time to brush my teeth, change my clothes, and get my notebook and pencil ready.

I ran to the open laptop my parents had set up for me on the kitchen table with thirty seconds to spare.

Moments later, my beautiful nani's

face popped up on the screen. Her salt and pepper, curly hair was tied back. Her soft brown eyes shone through the screen. Her face glowed when she saw me.

"Divya beta, I've missed you so much!" she said. "I am so happy to see your smiling face. It has been so long since we spoke. This time difference is too much! When I am awake you are getting ready to sleep. When I am asleep, you are getting ready to wake up. We barely get to talk. But never mind, I'm just so happy. Are you eating enough? How are your studies going? Is it very cold outside? I hear the weather is very cold where you are."

My sweet nani. I never noticed, but maybe I got my chatty personality from her. She was talking so quickly. Just like me.

"Nani, slow down. You are talking just as fast as me." I laughed. "I'm great. School is great. I'm eating, but I sure miss your cooking. Especially your ladoos. Which is why I am calling. Our class is having a bake sale to raise money for an outdoor classroom. I really want to make your super delicious ladoos."

Nani clapped her hands in front of her. "Oh, beta, nothing would make me happier! Let me think. I never write my recipes down. I just know what goes into the food by the look and smells." Nani looked up and rubbed her chin. "Well, do you have a pencil and paper?"

"I'm ready." I held up my notebook and pencil to show her I came prepared. "I really want to make these on my own and show everyone how responsible I am."

"Beta, I'm sure everyone already knows. Just know, you can always ask for help. Now tell me, do you want to make the boondi ladoos, the ones that are bright orange? They are a bit tricky and require some deep

frying. Or the besan ladoos, the light orange ones? They might be better as they are easier to make."

"I love them both. I love all ladoos, as you know. The besan are perfect. Let's do those," I said.

"Okay," said Nani, "first you will want to fry the besan in the ghee on low heat in the frying pan until the dough becomes darker orange and begins to smell delicious."

"*Mmmmm . . . ,*" I said. "I love that smell!" I knew exactly what Nani was talking about. The nutty smell of the chickpea flour always filled our home when she made ladoos.

Nani continued while I wrote so fast my hand hurt. "I like to add a good amount of powdered sugar, maybe half a cup. And about half a teaspoon of elaichi, which is cardamom that needs to be ground into powder."

"Okay," I said, "got it."

Nani continued, "And my most secret ingredient is saffron. I add about half a teaspoon of it. It gives the ladoos the most delicious flavor!"

My mouth watered. I couldn't wait to show everyone how good these ladoos were. When it was time to say goodbye, I wrapped my arms around the laptop while Nani did the same. It wasn't the same as hugging her in real life, but it was still nice. I promised to talk to her soon.

Note to self:

- ☆ I wonder if Nani can feel my hug from so far away?
- ☆ Schedule more calls with Nani on Saturday mornings.

Later that day, Mumma drove me to the Indian grocery store. It was the only Indian grocery store in our area. I hadn't been there yet, and my toes tingled in anticipation.

Mumma parked the car and started to get out.

"Mumma, I really want to do this on my own," I said. "Do you think you can wait in the car or maybe at the front door? I have my list ready. All I need is a bit of money." I put out my hand and smiled as big as I could in the hope she would say yes.

Mumma lifted her eyebrows. "Wow, Divya, you *are* serious about doing this on your own. Okay, I'll wait by the door." She reached into her purse. After some rummaging around, she took out some money and placed it in my outstretched hand.

As we walked through the front door, a bell chimed. It was gentle, like the ones in India. The smell of agarbatti tickled my nose. It was the same smell that greeted us in mandirs and like the one Dadi lit when she did her prayers in the morning.

The shelves were lined with products I had only seen in India. Each corner of the small store was stacked with groceries. The smells, the foods, the people shopping—they all reminded me of home.

"I'll wait here and look through the new selection of magazines while you shop, beta. Good luck! I'm here if you need me." Mumma turned toward the magazines lining the wall closest to the entrance. Each cover was filled with the latest Hindi movie star.

I waved at Mumma. I pulled a small shopping cart from beside the wall, and opened up my notebook.

After scanning my shopping list, I moved through the narrow aisles. I stopped at the aisle with floor-to-ceiling atta. Wow! I'd never seen so many different types of flour outside of India before. Where could the besan be?

I scanned the shelves, atta, whole wheat, channa, ragi, corn, the different types of flour seemed never ending until I finally saw it! Besan! I lifted the heavy bag and placed it into my cart.

Besan—check!

I moved to the next aisle and stopped. The most beautiful diyas—yellow, light blue, pink—covered with crystals were staring at me. They would be perfect as a mehndi party decoration!

I looked at the price and calculated how much money I had left. Just enough! I placed one of each color into my cart and smiled. I could just picture them glowing on the table.

Now back to my list of ingredients!
I looked to see what I needed:

- ✅ besan
- ☆ ghee (Dadi has some freshly made at home)
- ☆ elaichi
- ☆ saffron

I walked toward the spice aisle. My nose was overcome with sweet, earthy, spicy, and peppery aromas. The smells of cooking and the smells of home. *Mmmm* . . . delicious!

I recognized the elaichi right away. Nani used to offer me some after our meals together. It was hard to describe what it tasted like. Maybe if I combined mint, pepper, and flowers together, that might do.

My mouth watered. I picked up a small bag and put it into my cart. I couldn't wait to peel the pod and turn the seeds into powder.

But saffron was a whole different story. Nani never said much about saffron. What did it look like?

I carefully read the labels on each shelf and stopped when I got to the one that said "saffron." Aha! I looked up and stopped. It was empty! Where could it be? I asked a lady that worked at the store.

"Excuse me, aunty ji. Is there any saffron in the back? I can't seem to find it." I pointed to the empty space on the shelf.

"Beta, let me check." She walked through a door in the back and returned minutes later. "Sorry, we must be all out. Come back in a few weeks. We will surely have some by then."

My heart dropped. Nani's special ingredient! I slowly walked through the aisle toward the checkout. I paid for the groceries and put everything into a bag.

Everything had gone perfectly until the

missing saffron! What would I do now? I looked down at my shoes and slowly walked toward the exit.

Mumma met me at the door.

"Divya, did you get everything you need?" she asked. "You look so sad. Did everything go okay?"

I looked up at her and then down again. "Almost everything. The grocery store didn't have saffron. It was Nani's special ingredient. Now my ladoos won't be as good as Nani's," I whispered.

"Ah, I see. Well, I have good news for you. We have saffron at home! It's the red spice in the spice tin. You know the round steel tin in the kitchen drawer with the clear lid. It's just like the tin we had at home back in India."

The spice tin! Of course! This was the answer to my problem. I ran into her arms and hugged her. "Thanks, Mumma. I'm sooo happy."

Note to self:

☆ The Indian grocery store has *almost* everything!

☆ Between the ladoo and the decorations, it's my time to shine!

☆ I can't wait for tomorrow!

Chapter 7

The Preparation

"Dear family, I have the most wonderful surprise for you all," I said in between bites of my soggy cereal. "Please join me here promptly at 4 p.m." I used my loudest and clearest adult voice.

My tummy had fluttered with excitement since I woke up half an hour ago. It was time to put my supersecret plan into action.

"I can't wait to see what you are up to Divya. I have lots of homework to do today. But you know I'm always happy to ignore it to help you out if you need me," Sumeer said, looking at me with wide eyes pleading for me to accept his offer.

Taya and Tayi Ji glared at him. "I'm okay, thanks though," I laughed.

In between bites of toast, Geeta Didi said, "I'm going over to my friend's house to practice my dance moves, but I can come back early to help if you need me."

It was nice that they all wanted to help, but maybe they thought I couldn't do this on my own. I would show them . . .

"Thank you all, but like I've said, I've got this. Besides, it wouldn't be a surprise if you all helped!" I giggled.

Papa, who was sitting beside me, leaned over and whispered, "When did you grow up so much that you are surprising your parents? To me, you are still my little Divya."

I smiled. "Papa, I'm more grown up than

you know. I just can't wait to show you how much," I whispered back.

<u>Note to self:</u>

☆ Maybe I'll always be little to my parents, but I don't feel so little anymore.

I stacked all the ingredients I needed onto the kitchen counter.

The clock on the wall showed I had an hour before Asima came over at 3 p.m. Soon after, everyone would arrive at 4 p.m.

Dadi stood by the entrance and watched me wash my hands.

"Beta, are you sure I can't help you?" she asked. "I think everyone else can go, but I should stay. I can be here by your side

and hand you what you need. Like your assistant."

I looked at my sweet dadi. My nani would probably have done the same, watched me from the door. For a moment, I was tempted but then remembered my plan.

"Dadi, you know how much I love spending time with you, but I really want to do this on my own. Maybe you can finish knitting that scarf you were working on or even take your afternoon nap?"

I gently steered her in the direction of her room. "Okay, beta, I really should lie down while the house is quiet. You know where to find me." She walked into her room and lay down on her bed.

I gently closed the door and walked back to the kitchen.

I began by carefully measuring the besan and putting it to the side, just like Nani said. Then I melted the ghee on low heat. I had promised Mumma I would keep the heat low and be *extra* careful, which I always was. Then I mixed the besan and ghee together. So far so good! The air filled with the buttery smell Nani talked about.

I peeled the green elaichi pod and removed the black seeds from the inside. I placed the black seeds in the rounded bowl of the mortar and pounded them with the pestle until they were a powder. The air filled with the minty fragrance of the elaichi.

Everything was going so smoothly. Maybe I should cook and bake more. Maybe even start my own baking business! This really was a lot of fun.

I lifted the cover of the spice tin and looked for the red saffron. Mumma said this is where it was kept.

I stopped and my mouth dropped. Sitting side by side were two red spices. One red and powdery and the other red and stringy.

What should I do?

Okay, Divya. Think. What would saffron look like?

One of these has to be saffron, and there is no way saffron could be these small threads. They looked like one hundred teeny-tiny shoelaces! I picked up a thread and examined it between my fingers. My fingers turned slightly red. There is no way that this was Nani's special ingredient.

I turned to the other red powder in the spice box and it looked like the elaichi powder I just made. This must be it! I took a teaspoon and added a bit more than Nani suggested to make my ladoos extra special. I carefully mixed it into the dough.

After all the round-shaped ladoos were ready, I stood back and looked at all the delicious treats I made. I wanted so badly to take a bite, but I knew that if I did, I wouldn't be able to stop at just one, and they would all be gobbled up. Sumeer loved ladoos just as much as I did. He should have the honor of trying the first one!

Knock, knock. I looked up at the clock. It was exactly 3 p.m. and Asima had arrived. Perfect timing!

I washed my hands, gave the ladoos one last loving look, and turned my attention to part two of my plan. Time to decorate!

"Wow, everything looks amazing, if I do say so myself," Asima stepped back from the table and looked at all the work we had done.

The pink sheer glittering dupatta in the middle of the table looked magical on top of the white tablecloth. The diyas from the Indian grocery store were in a row across the table.

The bangles I brought from my bedroom were resting beside the diyas.

"Everything is so beautiful, but the backdrop is the most beautiful." I stepped back to admire our work.

Asima and I spent most of our time pinning up cascading dupattas from the top of the wall to the bottom. The combination of Geeta Didi's and my dupattas looked like a waterfall of blues, reds, and greens behind the table.

Asima used her hand to flatten out a bump on the table. "Your family will love it and will definitely use your ideas for the mehndi party decorations."

"I just know Simran Aunty will love it. I really want the day to be special for her." I placed the last orange bangle next to the yellow diya. The most perfect plate of freshly made ladoos was placed at the center of the table.

"Divya, I hate to do this, but I can't stay. My baba is picking me up any minute. I completely forgot that we are going to my cousin's house for dinner tonight."

I nodded. I wish my best friend was staying to celebrate with us but I knew she had to go. "Oh Asima, I was really hoping you could stay! But I understand." I wrapped my arms around her to give her a hug. "I couldn't have done this without you."

She hugged me back. I walked her to the door. "Everything looks perfect! I can't wait to hear how it goes. Call me and tell me everything!"

After our goodbyes, she was gone.

I looked at my watch again. My guests would be arriving soon.

Note to self:

☆ The butterflies in my tummy are out of control!

Chapter 8

The Disaster

"Divya beta, what is all this?" Dadi's eyes admired the decoration. "When did you plan this beautiful party?"

Before I could respond, a loud booming voice came closer. "Wah! What do we have here?" Taya Ji said walking into the dining room. Tayi Ji, Mumma and Papa were close behind him. They looked around the room with the same awe as Dadi.

"Divya, my dear, when did you do all this? This must have taken hours to prepare. Look at those delicious ladoos on the table too." Tayi Ji said in wonder.

Papa puffed his chest out in pride. "So, this was the surprise. Wow, beta, everything looks beautiful. You have outdone yourself."

Sumeer and Geeta Didi walked in moments later. My family, who were usually late, were so prompt today.

"So, this is the surprise you wanted us to see. These decorations look beautiful. And our dupattas look amazing." Geeta Didi gave me a wink. "The restaurant is nice, but these decorations would really make Simran Aunty's mehndi party extra special. Let me add, this is what Divya was trying to tell you last week. The restaurant can use a little something special for this event."

I smiled so wide the sides of my mouth hurt. I couldn't remember the last time I felt this good. Everything was going perfectly.

"Yes, these decorations look just like the kind we see in India. They would be perfect for the mehndi party. Great work, Divya,"

Mumma said. She lifted up one of the diyas and touched the crystals on the sides. "Did you get these at the Indian grocery store yesterday?"

I nodded.

"I'm going to see if I can buy a few more diyas for the mehndi party tomorrow after school," Mumma announced. "Divya, do you want to come with me?"

My toes tingled. "I would love that."

Sumeer walked to the table. "Sooo, I know you are all talking about these decorations, but all I see are ladoos. After Divya, I am the second best ladoo taster. I think it's time we give these a try."

I nodded. "I know you will love them."

Sumeer picked up the plate and offered everyone a round ball of deliciousness. Each person took one.

"These feel soft, but not too soft. Just the perfect texture," Sumeer said. He gave them a gentle squeeze. He put the plate down and stood behind the table just in front of the waterfall of dupattas.

"Eat up, everyone. I can't promise that there will be any left." Sumeer dropped the whole ladoo into his wide-open mouth while everyone else took a much smaller bite.

I sucked in a large breath. I expected him to tell me how delicious they were, how sweet and soft, but that didn't happen. Instead, Sumeer had a funny look on his face. The one where it looked like someone was tickling his nose with a feather, like he was about to sneeze. But it took forever to happen. And then finally,

"Aaachhhooooo!"

"Aaachooooo!"

He began sneezing out of control.

Papa hid a look of worry before he met my eyes. "Hmmm . . . Spicier than I remember but still good."

"Not bad . . . I might add more sugar next time," Tayi Ji said quickly.

My heart sank. I looked down at the ladoo in my hand.

What could have gone wrong? I opened my mouth to take a small bite and the red-hot taste of chili hit my taste buds with a wham. These definitely didn't taste like Nani's ladoos. They didn't even taste like ladoos at all. I looked around the room while the adults tried to smile. Geeta Didi hid half her ladoo in a tissue.

"I need water, I can't handle spice. Ladoos are supposed to be sweet." Sumeer waved his hands in front of his mouth. He leaned his head back, preparing for another sneeze. "*Aaachoooo!*"

Before I knew it, his hand got caught in the dupatta behind him. Without any warning, the dupattas from the wall tumbled to the floor and landed in a pile at my feet.

I looked around me.

Paused.

And ran to my room.

Note to self:

☆ This day went from being perfect, to the perfect disaster.

Chapter 9

The Mistake

How could this happen? What did I do wrong? Why did the ladoos taste so spicy? How could I have let everyone down? No one will remember my decorations now. And my ladoos were not ready for the bake sale. This was a disaster.

I threw myself on my bed and angry tears ran down my face.

I heard a knock, and before I could tell them I wanted to be alone, my family walked into the room. Sumeer cradled a big glass of water in his hands.

I sat up and wiped my face with my sleeve.

Mumma sat beside me and wrapped her arms around my shoulder. "Divya, beta, please don't be so upset. Everything was beautiful. The ladoos were very good. And you made them all on your own. We are so proud of you."

I looked down. "Everything was a disaster. My decorations are a mess and the ladoos are horrible."

"Beta, the decorations were beautiful. You have so many great ideas. We should have listened to you sooner," Tayi Ji said.

Taya Ji nodded. "Yes, beta, we were so focused on the food that we didn't listen to you. We love what you did and want to ask you to help us set up for Ms. Simran's party next weekend."

I looked up and found everyone looking at me. "I would like that," I said. "I just don't understand what happened with the ladoos. There were two red spices in the spice box. One was red and stringy and the other was a red powder. I didn't know which one was saffron so I guessed. I think I made the wrong choice. I should have just asked. But I just really wanted to do this all on my own to show you how responsible I was."

"Beta, that was our fault. I want you to know you should never be afraid to ask for help," Papa said. "We didn't listen to you when you shared your wonderful ideas. So sorry about that."

Dadi stepped forward. "Beta, your ladoos were good. I think you used red chili powder in place of red saffron. Otherwise, your ladoos were great. They will be ready for the bake sale in no time."

No wonder the ladoos were so spicy! The red powder was chili powder! And saffron was red and stringy! A smile slowly spread across my face. "Yes, no one should eat what I just made. But by the time the bake sale comes, we will make the best ladoos together."

Note to self:

☆ I guess it's okay to ask for help.

☆ Adults should listen to kids more.

Chapter 10

The Bake Sale

I removed the lid of the storage container and peeked inside. One hundred perfectly round, sweet, light orange ladoos sat neatly on top of one another.

I thought back to the last few days. With the help of Sumeer, Geeta Didi, and Dadi, we rolled each one out by hand. The saffron, instead of the chili, made them just right. Nani would be so proud.

Note to self:

☆ Tell Nani how delicious her ladoos are on our next video call.

☆ Tell her that red chili powder is not a good substitute for saffron!

When I got to the gymnasium, I found the sign that read, "Ms. Yang's Fourth Grade Bake Sale." I walked up to the table and Ms. Yang greeted me.

"Thank you for this wonderful idea, Divya," she said. "I think our bake sale will be a huge hit. Look at all these treats. I want to buy each and every one of them for myself."

I laughed. "Wait until you see my ladoos. I bet you can't eat just one."

Ms. Yang laughed.

Asima was standing just behind Ms. Yang, and I walked over to her. "I see another family. I'll let you both chat like

usual," Ms. Yang said, walking away to greet them.

I smiled proudly and placed my container on the table right next to Asima's. Her ma'amoul sat on a big serving dish.

"Asima, your cookies look delicious," I said. "I brought my money and can't wait to try some."

"And don't forget mine," Jamal said as he placed his toffee-like treats next to ours.

Sumeer's fourth-grade class had a table across from ours. Handmade cards were displayed all over. I saw Sumeer's right away. His was the brightly colored card with a lime green car on the front. Sumeer was huddled in a corner talking to his friends.

I waved at him, and he waved back.

The music in the gymnasium was blasting, and from the corner of my eye I saw Geeta Didi dancing with her friends. I know she said she wasn't excited about a danceathon, but that smile on her face made me think she was having a good time.

After some time, Mr. Khan, the school principal walked toward the microphone set up in the corner of the gymnasium. "Good evening, everyone! We are excited to share that Family Fun night was a huge success and that we raised enough money for the outdoor classroom! Thank you all for your hard work." A cheer erupted from the crowd.

I looked around and saw my cousins happy, my friends trying each other's treats, and my family at the table buying handmade cards. With Simran Aunty's mehndi party on the weekend, the fun was going to continue.

Note to self:

☆ This is the best day ever!

Glossary

agarbatti (ay-gar-BAHT-ee)—incense sticks

aloo paratha (uh-LOO puh-RAH-thuh)—a flatbread stuffed with spiced mashed potatoes

besan (BEH-suhn)—flour made of ground chickpeas

beta (BEY-tuh)—a Hindi nickname meaning *my child*

chai (CHYE)—tea made with spices and milk

diya (DEE-yuh)—a small oil lamp made from clay or mud

dupatta (duh-PAH-tuh)—a long shawl-like scarf

elaichi (ee-LYE-chee)—a spice made from the seed pods of the cardamom plant

ghee (GEE)—a kind of liquid butter

ma'amoul (mah-ah-MOOL)—a butter cookie with a filling of dried fruit or nuts

mehndi party (MEN-dee PAR-tee)—a pre-wedding party where the bride's hands and feet are decorated with henna dye

namaste (NUHM-uh-stay)—a respectful greeting

salwar kameez (SAL-war kuh-MEEZ)—a traditional Indian outfit

Thinking About the Story

☆ Divya felt like her ideas weren't taken seriously by the adults around her. Think about a time when you felt your voice may not have been heard. How did you feel? What did you do? Who supported you along the way? Who or what helped you get through it?

☆ Divya was really excited about Simran Aunty's mehndi party being held at Delhi Delights and the fundraiser for the outdoor classroom. What are some things you are excited about at home or school? Make a list. How can you share this with those around you so they can know you better?

☆ Speak to your family about a recipe that has been in the family for years and share it with your class. This project can even be made in a class recipe book!

☆ How do you think Divya felt when she realized her mistake about mixing up saffron with chili powder in her ladoo? Write an encouraging letter to Divya about what she may have learned through this experience.

Make Ladoo!

I bet you would love to taste my special ladoo Good news: with this recipe, you can! Be sure to ask a grown up for permission and for help along the way. After all, you don't want to end up with super spicy ladoo!

What You Need:

- 1½ cup of besan, (chickpea flour)
- about ⅓ cup of ghee (clarified butter)
- about ½ teaspoon of ground elaichi (cardamom)
- ½ teaspoon of saffron
- about ⅓ cup of powdered sugar
- sliced almonds, optional (to be placed on top of each ladoo)

What You Do:

1. Use a sieve to sift the besan so it is not clumpy. Set it aside.

2. Put the ghee in a heavy pan on low heat and wait for it to melt.

3. Once the ghee melts, add the besan to the pan, which is still on low heat, and mix it together until it combines.

4. Keep mixing the besan and ghee for about 7 or 8 minutes until thoroughly combined. The dough will turn a darker orange-brown color and there will be a fragrant smell. That's when you know it is cooking correctly!

5. Remove the pan from the stove and mix in the elaichi powder and saffron.

6. Let the dough cool for 5 to 10 minutes and then mix in the sugar.

7. Keep mixing until the sugar is incorporated and the dough is smooth.

8. Form into little balls and add almonds on top.

9. They are ready to eat. Enjoy!

About the Creators

Sita Jit is a children's book author and elementary school teacher. Just like Divya, she grew up close with her extended family in Canada and India. In her free time, Sita loves to read, listen to music, and play board games. She lives in Ontario with her husband and three children.

Abhilasha Khatri is a children's book illustrator based in India. She transitioned into the whimsical world of children's books after working as an architect for over a decade. She loves to work on multicultural, inclusive, and diverse stories. In her free time, Abhilasha loves gardening, traveling, DIY, cooking and baking, and playing with her daughter and her cats.

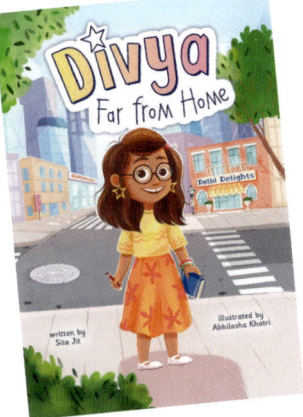

Check out their first Divya Dubey book!